OUR CLOTHES

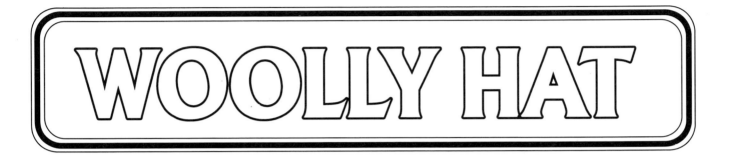

WOOLLY HAT

Wayne Jackman

Reading Consultant:
Diana Bentley
University of Reading

Commissioned photographs:
Chris Fairclough

Wayland

Our clothes

Denim Jeans
Leather Shoes
Nylon Tracksuit
Plastic Raincoat
Woolly Hat

Editor: Janet De Saulles

First published in 1990 by
Wayland (Publishers) Ltd
61 Western Road, Hove
East Sussex, BN3 1JD, England

British Library Cataloguing in Publication Data
Jackman, Wayne
  Woolly hat
  1. Wool
  I. Title II. Fairclough, Chris III. Series
  677'.31

  ISBN 1–85210–856–8

Phototypeset by Rachel Gibbs, Wayland.
Printed and bound by Casterman S.A., Belgium

Contents

All the words that appear
in **bold** are explained in the
glossary on page 22.

Where does wool come from?

Do you wear a woolly hat in the winter? The children in the photograph do. Wool is very cosy and keeps us warm. People have made clothes from wool for thousands of years. Most of the wool we use comes from sheep. Many different **breeds** of sheep are found all over the world.

Right *Have you got a woolly hat?*

4

Left We get wool from animals such as these sheep in New Zealand.

Below Would you like to have your clothes made with wool from these angora goats?

Some of our wool comes from other animals such as the mohair goat, the angora rabbit or the llama. Like sheep, these animals have woolly coats. We do not use these types of wool very much though because they are more expensive than wool from sheep.

Above *Wool from lambs is extra warm and soft.*

Shearing the sheep

To get the wool from sheep the **fleece** must be cut off. This is called shearing. It does not hurt the sheep at all – it is a bit like when you have your hair cut. Nowadays, quick electric clippers are used. An expert **shearer** can clip about 150 sheep each day. Shearing usually takes place in spring or summer when the sheep no longer need their thick coats to keep warm.

Right *This sheep shearer from New Zealand is using electric clippers.*

6

Sometimes hand clippers are used. They look like large scissors and are much slower to use than the new electric clippers.

After shearing the wool is sorted into **grades**. Different sheep produce different grades of wool. Any dirty or ragged wool is removed and the rest is weighed and **baled up**. It is then sent for sale by auction.

Below These children are helping to bale the wool on a farm in Australia.

Below Big machines are used to card the wool.

8

When the wool arrives at the factory it is still full of dust, mud, thistles, seeds and grease. To get rid of these, the wool is washed in warm, soapy water. The wool is now ready to be dyed. White wool is easier to dye than black wool. This is why black sheep are not kept so much nowadays.

After being washed and dyed the wool is all tangled up. It is straightened out by a carding machine which is like a giant hair-brush. It brushes the thousands of wool **fibres** and straightens them out just like you do after you wash your hair. Sometimes the wool is also put through a combing machine. This removes all the short and broken fibres.

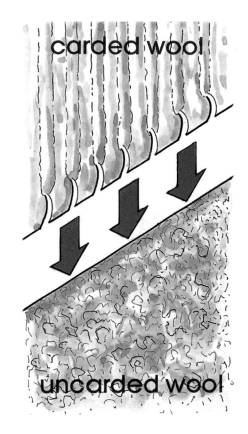

carded wool

uncarded wool

Above This diagram shows what wool looks like before and after being carded.

Above *Wool being spun by machine.*
Opposite page *These German children are wearing snowsuits and hats made from woollen cloth.*

Spinning

After combing the wool, the next step is to join together the thousands of wool fibres into one long thread. The wool fibres have rough, scaly edges. This helps them lock on to each other as they are twisted together. This twisting process is called spinning.

In some parts of the world spinning is done by hand. In other parts, the carded and combed wool is fed into special spinning machines. These stretch and twist the fibres, joining them together to make one long thread called yarn. The yarn is then wound on to **bobbins** ready to be made into woollen cloth.

Above *Do you think that the jumpers these children are wearing have been knitted by hand or on a machine?*

Weaving and knitting

One way of making woollen fabric is knitting. Have you ever seen knitting being done by hand? In factories huge knitting machines are used which work in the same way as hand knitting but are much faster. The needles make loops in the wool yarn and thread them together in rows.

Right *This Irish woman is knitting with a hand knitting machine.*

Look at the diagram on this page. Can you see how the yarn is threaded under and over? This is called weaving. Weaving can be done by hand on hand looms or by machine on big mechanical looms.

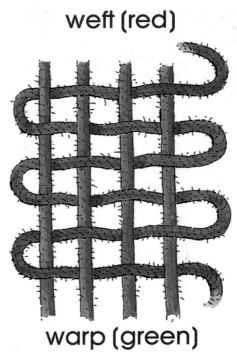

weft (red)

warp (green)

Above This diagram shows how weaving is done.

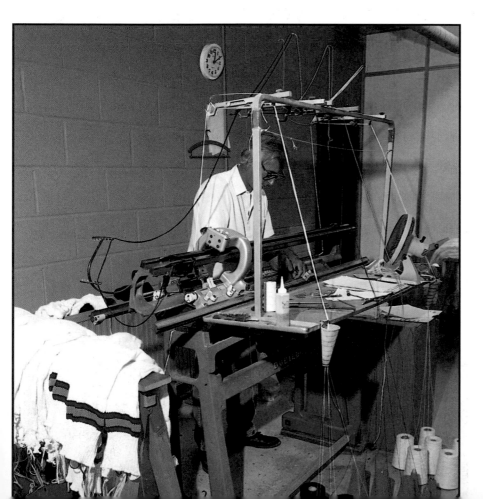

Left Cricket pullovers being knitted.

Above *Special types of sewing machines are used to sew pieces of cloth together.*

Opposite page
Whether we are working or playing, wool keeps us warm and comfortable.

Turning cloth into clothes

The woollen cloth and knitted fabric can now be made into clothes. First of all, patterns for the clothes must be designed and drawn up. The cloth is then cut out using these patterns. The various pieces are passed along to **machinists** who sew them together. Finally they are pressed and inspected.

Some clothes, though, are not made by machine in a factory. They are made by hand. The cloth must then be cut and sewn so that it will fit the person exactly.

Below *Here are some of the stages that wool must go through before it is made into a woolly hat.*

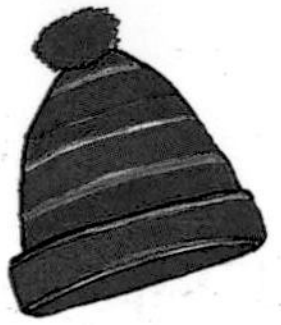

The woolly hat is now finished

The pictures on these pages show how your woolly hat is made. Wool is one of the best fibres to use for many of our clothes because it keeps the warmth inside near our skin and makes us feel cosy. It is also strong

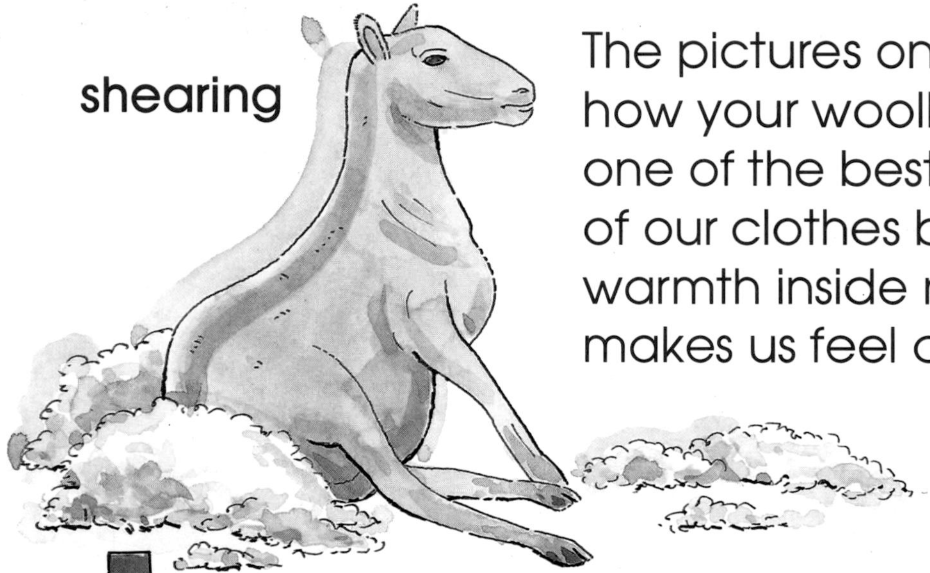

shearing

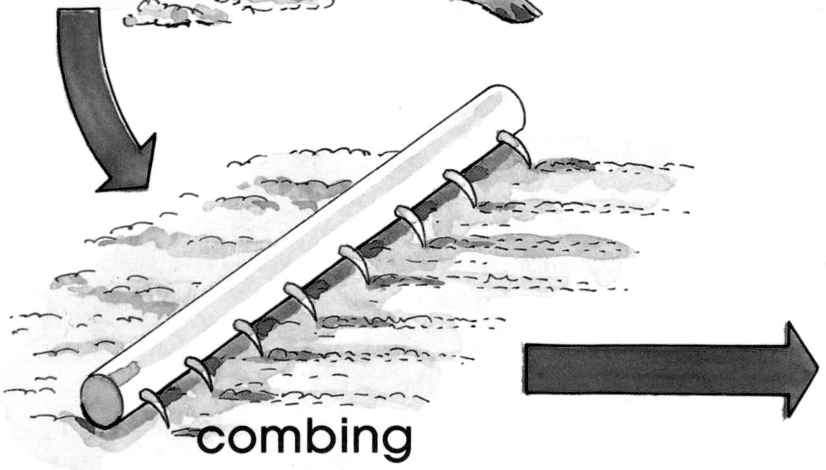

combing

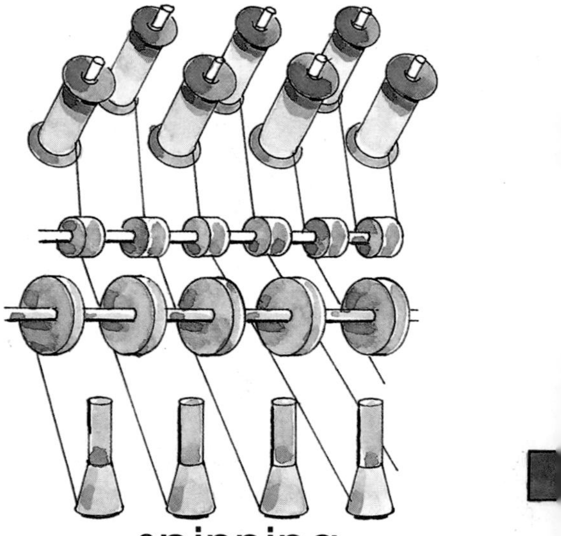

spinning

and lasts a long time. If wool is stretched it will spring back into shape.

Another reason why wool is useful is that it can soak up water – or sweat if we get too hot. This makes it ideal for sportswear. Finally, wool does not burn easily, so woollen clothing is very useful where there is any danger of fire.

finished hat

knitting

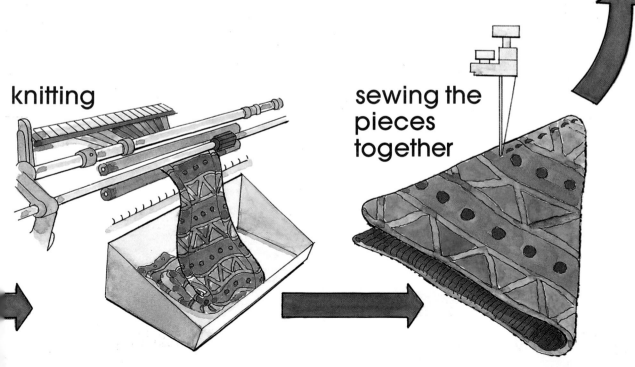

sewing the pieces together

Above *We must wash our woollen clothes carefully. If the water is too hot the wool may shrink.*

Some things made from wool

Many things are made from wool. One way of recognizing them is by looking out for the wool symbol. How many sorts of clothes can you think of that are made of wool?

Wool is not only used for clothes. It has many other uses. Are you standing on a carpet? Maybe it is a warm woollen carpet or perhaps it is a beautiful woollen rug from Turkey or India. Wool can also be used for car seat covers, wallpaper, curtains, pillows, duvets, shoe linings and even tennis balls!

Above *The wool symbol tells us that something is made from 100 per cent pure wool.*

Left *How many things made of wool can you see in this picture?*

Wool games and experiments

Look for something that you think is made of wool. Does it have a wool symbol on the label? Now rub it on your cheek. If it does not feel soft, bouncy and warm it is not wool.

Next, try the dampness test. Put on one woollen glove and one made of **man-made** fibre. Wet them both. After five minutes the wool glove will feel dryer than the other.

You could maybe ask someone to teach you to knit. You could even try knitting a woolly hat!

Below *Woollen clothes can be made in many different colours.*

Left *How soft this wool feels!*

Below *Wool is very strong – it will not break if you pull it.*

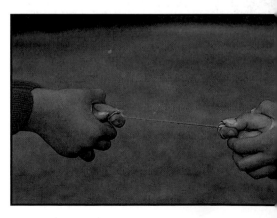

21

Glossary

Baled up   When wool is put into large bags and tied up.

Bobbins   Objects which you wind thread round ready to be used later.

Breeds   Types or sorts of animal.

Fibres   Little hair-like threads.

Fleece   The woolly coat of a sheep.

Grades   Levels of something. A high grade is good, a low grade is bad.

Machinists   People who use sewing machines to make clothes.

Magnified   When something is made to look bigger using a special piece of glass.

Man-made   Something which is not found in nature.

Shearer   The person who shears the sheep.

Books to read

A First Look at Cloth by Robin Kerrod (Franklin
    Watts 1974)
Children's Clothes by Miriam Moss (Wayland
    1988)
Focus on Wool by Andrew Langley (Wayland
    1985)
How Clothes are Made by Sue Crawford
    (Wayland 1987)
How it's Made: Clothing and Footwear by
    Donald Clarke (Marshall Cavendish 1978)
Wool by Annabelle Dixon (A. & C. Black 1988)

Acknowledgements

The author and Publisher would like to thank the Headmistress and staff of Davigdor
Infant School, Hove, East Sussex, for all their help in the production of this book.

They would also like to thank the following for allowing their illustrations to be reproduced
in this book: The International Wool Secretariat 8, 10; Wayland Picture Library 12 (both), 15
and 20; Zefa 11. The illustrations on pages 9, 13, 16, 17 and 19 are by Stephen Wheele.

Index